WOMEN AND LUNA

the moon
goddess

*Edited by John Miller
and Tim Smith*

CHRONICLE BOOKS
SAN FRANCISCO

Printed in Singapore.

Library of Congress Cataloging-in-Publication Data:
The Moon goddess / edited by John Miller & Tim Smith.
        p.   cm.
ISBN 0-8118-1128-X
1. Moon—Literary collections. 2. Women—
Literary collections. I. Miller, John, 1959-   .
II. Smith, Tim, 1962-   .

    PN6071.M6M664   1995
808.8'036—dc20   95-12953
                                    CIP

Editing and design: Big Fish Books
Composition: Jennifer Petersen, Big Fish Books

Distributed in Canada by Raincoast Books,
8680 Cambie Street, Vancouver, B.C. V6P 6M9

10 9 8 7 6 5 4 3 2 1

Chronicle Books
275 Fifth Street
San Francisco, CA 94103

THANKS TO

KIRSTEN MILLER

SHELLEY BERNIKER

REGAN CLARKE

Contents

SASHA FENTON

*The Goddess
of the Moon*

The Moon in mythology and in many religions represents the female force which reflects the male force of the Sun. In Hebrew she is known as Levanah, in Roman mythology Diana and in the Greek tradition as Persephone and also Aphrodite. In the Egyptian tradition she is Isis the female member of the powerful trinity of Osiris, Isis and Horus.

To the followers of the ancient traditions of witchcraft, she is Brid, Maiden-Goddess of the waxing Moon; Diana, Mother-Goddess of the full Moon and Morrigan, Crone-

Goddess of the waning Moon. The following lines are an extract from a ritual associated with the Moon Goddess.

Behold is the Three-Formed Goddess:

She who is ever Three—Maid,

    Mother and Crone.

Yet she is ever One;

She in all women, and they all in her.

Behold her, remember her,

Forget not one of her faces;

If you would like the goddess to grant you a wish, then take a piece of paper in the planetary colour of the person (or object) that your wish concerns; then light the candle and wait for it to burn down, as it does so, the spell will be working. Here is the invocation which will help the spell to work.

Upon this candle will I write

What I request of thee this night.

Grant what I wish you to do;

I dedicate this rite to you.

I trust that you will grant this boon

O lovely Goddess of the Moon.

Early man's initial concern was to survive. In some parts of the world even now where life is primitive, survival is still not guaranteed. For such people, the business of growing food and rearing animals went alongside the development of the calendar and also the development of religion and superstition. If an offering to a particular deity would help the crops grow; then obviously, that was the right thing to do. Even now, many good people like to say grace before or after a

meal to thank God for feeding them. Even a total hea-
then such as I simply cannot eat the first fruits and veg-
etables of the season without offering up a Hebrew
blessing.

Most religions take some account of the Moon's
position in their festival calendar; for instance, in the
Christian tradition, Easter and Whitsun still "float"
according to the Moon's orbit. It is interesting to note
that Easter was a Greco-Roman festival associated with
Aphrodite and Diana and, before that a festival associated with Ishtarte, the predecessor of Aphrodite/Diana.
These goddesses, like the beginning of the spring season
itself, speak of fertility and growth and the renewal of life.
If you can take a trip to the re-discovered city of Ephesus in Turkey, just at the bottom of the hill on the left-
hand side you will find the Temple of Diana which is
close by the even more ancient site of the Temple of

Aphrodite/Ishtarte. Ishtarte is the many-breasted God-dess of Fertility who was sometimes shown hung about with eggs—Easter eggs perhaps?

In the Jewish tradition, special prayers are said when festivals fall at the time of the New Moon (Boruha Levanah), prayers for each new Moon are said at the beginning of the lunar month (Rosh Hadesh). Astrologers watch the Moon carefully and there are some who will not even discuss a new project on a "void of course Moon" which is when the Moon makes no major aspects to other planets. It is my guess that in all traditions and beliefs the Sun and Moon were, are and always will be the light which makes us turn our heads to the sky and our thoughts heavenwards.

The image of the Moon as the supreme female, the complete mother, is strongly represented in the Egyptian goddess, Isis, who presided over herbal remedies and

Lunar magic. If you wish to invoke the goddess Isis, draw a circle late at night, concentrate your thoughts and visualize an image of the goddess while asking for what you want. Above all, ask for the love and strength to be able to cope with your troubles and live a kindly and decent life. Here is a tiny extract from The Worship of Isis rituals.

▶

And over these tides the Great Goddess presides under her aspect of the Moon. As she passeth from her rising to her setting, so answer these tides unto her. She riseth from the sea as the evening Star, and the waters of the earth rise in flood. She sinketh as Luna in the western ocean, and the waters flow back into the inner Earth and are still in that great lake of darkness wherein are the Moon and Stars reflected. Whoso is still as the dark underworld lake of Persephone shall see the tides of the Unseen moving therein and shall know all things. Therefore is Luna also called the giver of visions.

In the Kabbalistic tradition, the Moon, this time known as Levanah, is associated with the section of the Tree of Life which is called Yesod. Yesod, the Foundation, is situated towards the base of the Tree just above Malkuth. Yesod is the ninth path of pure intelligence and it purifies the emanations. Yesod contains two totally different images; the watery Moon of Levanah under the presidency of the water element archangel, Gabriel, and also the magical image of a beautiful naked young man who is known for his strength alongside the powerful God name of Shaddai el Chai, the Almighty living God. Nothing in the Kab-balah is easy to understand, but the idea behind Yesod is that the universe was a vaporous and watery chaos which was gathered into order by the strength and power of God. Genesis—Boraishis. Here is a Greco/Hebrew version of the Isis worship ritual.

▶

Our Lady is also the Moon, called of some Selene, of others Luna, but by the wise Levanah, for therein is contained the numbers of her name. She is the ruler of the tides and flux and reflux. The waters of the Great Sea answer unto her, likewise the tides of all earthly seas, and she ruleth the nature of women.

Whilst reading through the proofs of this section I decided to look a little more closely into the phrase "for therein is contained the number of her name." This led me into a fascinating line of research where I discovered that the "alphabet number" Hebrew letters for the names Levanah and

Luna were the same, e.g. lamed, vov, nun and hey. The numerology was, of course the same: 30, 6, 50, 5, making a total of 91[*]. I haven't had a chance yet to find an ancient Greek alphabet, but my guess is that when I

do Selene will turn out to have the same numeric value. This led me further into Hebrew Kabbalistic numerology, which had been a specialty of my grandfather's during his lifetime. This type of esoteric thinking is obviously beyond the scope of this book, but it just goes to show how much knowledge is wrapped up in these old sayings.

In Kabbalistic divination, Yesod rules the instincts, habit patterns, food, home environment, sex and sexual organs. This is also the wife in a male reading, and the ninth month of pregnancy.

---

[*] *True Hebrew numerology is like Roman numerology with some letters representing hundreds and thousands, etc.*

Before we leave the world of religion and magical belief I would like to advise you to perform all ritual and psychic work during daylight (except for the Isis invocation), even if you are only trying out ideas for size. This is because one's resistance is low after dark, and low-level entities may be drawn in due to the unbalanced forces of the Moon and your tired mind. If you are at all tuned in to your own lunar phases, then avoid doing any psychic work at those times when you know you will be at a low ebb. I know, for example, that I tend to feel tired, ratty and off-colour just after the new Moon each month, probably because I was born a couple of days after a full Moon.

Good luck with your magic, may the Goddess of the Moon guide your instincts towards greater understanding and the ability to help others along their paths towards enlightenment.

DRUID
INCANTATIONS

When I shall have departed from this world,

    Whenever you have need of anything,

Once in the month, and when the moon is full,

Ye shall assemble in some desert place

Or in a forest all together join

To adore the potent spirit of your Queen

My mother, great *Diana*. She who fain

Would learn all sorcery yet has not won

Its deepest secrets, them my mother will

Teach her, in truth all things as yet unknown.

And ye shall all be freed from slavery,

And so ye shall be free in everything;

And as a sign that ye are truly free,

Ye shall be naked in your rites, both men

And women also: this shall last until

The last of your oppressors shall be dead. . . .

ANNE SEXTON

Moon Song,
Woman Song

I am alive at night.
I am dead in the morning,
an old vessel who used up her oil,
bleak and pale boned.
No miracle. No dazzle.
I'm out of repair
but you are tall in your battle dress
and I must arrange for your journey.
I was always a virgin,

old and pitted.

Before the world was, I was.

I have been oranging and fat,

carrot colored, gaped at,

allowed my cracked o's to drop on the sea

near Venice and Mombasa.

Over Maine I have rested.

I have fallen like a jet into the Pacific.

I have committed perjury over Japan.

I have dangled my pendulum,

my fat bag, my gold, gold,

blinkedy light

over you all.

So if you must inquire, do so.

After all I am not artificial.

I looked long upon you,

love-bellied and empty,

flipping my endless display

for you, you my cold, cold

coverall man.

You need only request

and I will grant it.

It is virtually guaranteed

that you will walk into me like a barracks.

So come cruising, come cruising,

you of the blast off,

you of the bastion,

you of the scheme.

I will shut my fat eye down,

headquarters of an area,

house of a dream.

FREDERICK ADAMS

Witchcraft Rites

All life on Earth participates in
the dance of Moon and Sun.
And we, engendered in the oceans,
feel in our blood the pull of
our Moon upon the tides.
We are sunlight transformed by
trees into fruit and plasm, and we
are so intimately of the Earth that
our collective dream is paradise.
Thus we are moved to celebrate
the ceaseless play of the seasons

and to ensoul ourselves,

landscape and heaven.

Our Earth, a very great Goddess in artistic communion with The Cosmic Korê, displays the magnificent pageant of the seasons. . . .

The year is a continual courtship between Moon and Sun. On May Day . . . Moon and Sun become engaged. At this time flowers are in full bloom. On the first day of Summer, They are married: fruits are forming. In the middle of Summer, Lammas, The Goddess and God are on Their Honeymoon: fruits are ripening.

On the first day of Autumn, Moon Goddess and Sun God come home: the fruits are dropping, crops being ingathered. At the middle of Autumn, Hallowe'en, the Divine Lovers prepare for the long Winter sleep of all Nature: leaves and seeds are settling to soil.

On the first day of Winter, Yule, the Goddess suddenly reawakens. She finds The God has mysteriously departed, but She is pregnant with The God of the coming year, really the same God, the Lord Sun Himself. . . . Yule is when the Sun starts North again, thus promising that Spring will follow the long cold rest period of Winter.

At the middle of the winter, Candlemas, The Goddess emerges from Her Royal Bedroom, The Great Earth-Sphere, and prepares to give birth to The Sun God again as an infant: enscaled buds stand out on bare branches.

Then, on the first day of Spring, Ostara, She does give birth to the baby Sun: fragile buds emerge from their scales in the dewy Sunrise of the year. The Goddess bathes in Her magic fountain and becomes a girl again. She and The God grow up together, very rapidly. Once more They become engaged on May Day, when buds are opening into flowers.

ZSUZSANNA BUDAPEST

The Dianic Traditions
and Rites of Life

CASTING THE CIRCLE

The Casting of the Circle is crucial for any ritual work. The ritual work must correlate the correct planetary aspects with the purpose of the work.

Gather the sisters participating in the ritual and measure a circle by holding each other's hands and standing at arm's length. Mark the circle by gathering a stone to replace one's foot space. Gather more stones and build an alter in the middle of the circle, slightly to the north (power corner). Upon the stone alter, set your representation of the Mother Goddess; an image, or a single rose, is fine. Place two white candles (one to the east, one to the west) of the Goddess image.

Each woman now places one white candle on the alter, and one on the outside circle stone.

Women are needed to mark out the circle with flour and barley, and write the names of the Goddess within the circle. They are also to consecrate the grounds with fire and air by walking around with incense in the circle (frankincense and myrrh are traditional; herbal incense is fine).

The High Priestess (HP) purifies all grounds and herself with water and salt (or seawater, if it is available). Her priestesses leave the circle to meditate. The HP draws the circle with her witch's knife on the ground in an uninterrupted way, separating the grounds of worship from the rest. It is drawn from east to south to west to north, leaving a gate to the east open for the women to enter.

Women gather to enter, oldest first, youngest last.

The HP sprinkles purifying water on each one, saying:

I purify you from all anxiety, all fears, in

the name of Diana.

Woman answers:

I enter the circle in perfect love and perfect trust.

HP kisses and embraces the woman.

Welcome to the Goddess's presence.

With incense, HP consecrates each woman with a pentagram in the air. Each woman then attends to lighting her candles on the alter and outer circle. When the last woman has entered, the HP closes the gate with her knife and says:

This circle is closed. The Goddess blesses Her women.

To unify: Form the circle with linked bodies, hands on napes of necks. Breathe deeply to oxygenate. Every woman makes a sound with her body that can manifest as a low hum, or Goddess names, or just variations of the sound the group uses.

Backing the HP, the women turn to the east, drawing a pentagram in the air with their witches' knives.

HP walks to the east corner, drawing a pentagram in the air with her athalme, kissing the blade after each invocation:

❯

(East:) *Hail to thee, powers of the East! Hail to the great eagle, corner of all beginnings! Ea, Astarte, Aurora, Goddess of all Beginnings! Come and be witness to our rite as we perform it according to ancient rites!*

(South:) *Hail to thee, powers of the South! Corners of great fire and passion, Goddess Esmeralda, Goddess Vesta and Heartha! Come and be witness at our rite as we perform it according to ancient laws!*

(West:) Hail to thee, powers of waters! Life-giving Goddess of the Sea, Aphrodite, Marianne, Themis, Tiamat! Come and guard our circle and bear witness to our rite as we perform it according to ancient rites!

(North:) Hail to thee, corner of all powers! Great Demeter, Persephone, Kore, Ceres! Earth Mothers and Fates! Great sea of glass! Guard our circle and bear witness as we perform our rite according to your heritage!

GENERAL RULES

Correlate your spells with the phases of the moon. On the waxing moon, do positive spells: love, health, money, success. The nine-day spells should land during the full moon, when boons are granted. On the waning moon, tie that which is loose, dispel evil, return bad vibes. Correlate your spells with the proper planets, if you can. Know the proper

name of the Goddess for the different aspects appropriate
for the spell. Remember, the Lady Who weaves our lives
has a certain pattern for all people to fulfill; if you find that
what you want is not to be, don't lose heart, but understand the Goddess has Veto power. Bless Her will, and
search for wisdom.

SPELL TO RAISE A STORM

This spell will help you raise a storm whenever one is
needed. It is usually done by a shaman who goes into a
field with her shaman drum and stands in front of a huge,
smoking fire, built for the occasion. She begins by drum-
ming up the spirits and singing:

Diana. . . Diana . . . Diana. . .

I am summoning forty-five spirits from the west!

I am summoning forty-five spirits from the east!

Bring now furies of hail, furies of water,

Their limbs with lightning afire,

Biting with water into our fields.

Enthroned Queens of fire,

The archers of the sacred bows and arrows,

The gatherers of rain from the wide skies,

Graciously be merciful to us!

Our fields and herbs with blessings keep safe!

Rains, rains, rains,

Give from your wide skies, burst water upon us!

Behold our wine in your chalice,

Accept our offerings to you!

Send the dark clouds over us,

Surround our fields with stormy rains.

You who wield the thunderbolts,

We call upon Thee!

Blessed be! Blessings be!

In some countries, the shamans draw moon symbols on the ground in flour and barley, then dance around them. If you need a really large storm, work on it for three consecutive evenings at dusk. Use wands instead of knifes, and instruments (drums, cymbals, rattles, anything) for making sounds to be shouted with great emotion and energy.

OLD HUNGARIAN HEALTH SPELL

When somebody is ill, and all the herbal medicines and the doctor's medicine seem to be no help, perform this as a last try.

Lay the ill person naked in a beam of full moonshine. Have one basket filled with thirteen fresh eggs and another basket that is empty. Take one egg at a time and rub it on the person's skin slowly, touching all the crevices. When the entire egg surface is used, take the next fresh egg and place the used one in the empty basket. While you do this, say:

> *By the power of Diana, by the power of Aradia, may*
> *all that is ill be absorbed into this egg. By the power*
> *of Queen Isis, so mote it be.*

When all thirteen eggs are used, take a little water, bless it, put salt in it, bless it again, and sprinkle it around the corners of the sick room, saying:

> *The Goddess blesses her child. All is well now.*
> *Fresh new health will glow.*

Dispose of the eggs in a living body of water, or bury them. Do not eat the eggs or you will get the illness.

SPELL TO REMOVE WARTS

Use a base of rose water; make your own, or buy it already prepared. Add a little fresh milkweed sap crushed from the stems of the plant, some dry crumbled mint leaves, sage, and sassafras leaves. Warm gently over a low flame. DO NOT BURN. Write on a piece of paper, and read aloud:

> Mother of seasons
>
> And the changing moon,
>
> Lady of light
>
> And giver of Spring−time,
>
> Give health to (name), our friend,
>
> And in the secret places of the night
>
> Make her/his warts dissolve,
>
> Not to return.
>
> Be with her/him
>
> And with us,
>
> Mother of the universe.

Burn the paper to ashes and add it to the mixture. When the mixture is warm and fragrant, BUT NOT HOT, put it in a small jar to cool. The patient should apply some at night before retiring, and let it dry. Leave it on all night and wash it off in the morning. Use faithfully each night until warts are completely dissolved.

THE DIANIC TRADITION

In the True Beginning, before the Judeo–Christian Genesis, the Goddess was revealed to her people as the Soul of the Wild. She was called Holy Mother, known to be a Virgin who lived in wild places and acted through mysterious powers. Known also as Artemis, She was worshipped in the moonlight, and young nymphs and maidens were called to serve in Her rituals. It was decreed that the sacred doe of Artemis was never to be shot down. The Holy Mother, Virgin, Artemis was also called by the name Dia Anna, "Nurturer Who Does Not Bear Young." In hunting and gathering societies Her image was carefully engraved in stone. She was symbolized by both the Sun and Moon to recognize that the torch of life and the healing Moon were Hers. Images of the Mother were carved everywhere She was worshipped: in caves, Yoni-shrines, the woods, trees. She was the Lady of Plenty, Teacher of Knowledge, Knower of Wisdoms, Sacred Dancer, Inventor of the Wheel, Holy Mother, Virgin, Artemis, Dianna.

In the Dianic times there were colleges of women who lived according to the spiritual principles of Artemis, serving in Her shrines and blessing the sick. Later, as knowledge of growing plants and domesticating animals was acquired, Artemis/Dianna became connected to all the people through Her sacred functions as Giver of Bread, Maker of the Loaf, Rainmaker and Life-Giver.

The worship of Dianna comes to us from these earliest Stone Age times. Her names appear throughout the world. The rivers Danube and Don were named after

Her. Ancient names for Anatolia, as well as current names for mountains, rivers and lakes worldwide, often reveal themselves in translation as Moon Goddess names from antiquity. Mt. St. Helens means Moonmountain. The most astonishing temples ever built (Stonehenge, for example) were created for the Moon Goddess.

Although most of the world's religions originated from the worship of the Moon Goddess, or "She Who Shines On All," Her worship and service were always carried out by women. While the Goddess as Giver of Life and Mother of the Sacred Child was worshipped by both sexes, Dianna was not. She was worshipped as Protector and Teacher of the Young, but never as a bearer of children; she did not consort with men. Her service was known as "Women's Mysteries," and ran parallel to worship of other Goddess aspects. Thus many women chose to worship the Goddess with their men, while many chose to worship alone or with each other. From the dawn of humankind, woman-energy as nurturing energy, expressed through Goddess-worship, has been strengthened through this very holy bonding.

◗

The Witch's Chant

Darksome night and shining Moon,
Hearken to the witches' rune.
East and South and West and North,
Hear! Come! I call Thee forth!

By all the powers of land and sea,
Be obedient unto me.
Wand and Pentacle and Sword,
Hearken ye unto my word.
Cord and Censer, Scourge and Knife,
Waken all ye into life.

Powers of all the Witches' Blade,

Come ye as the charge is made.

Queen of Heaven, Queen of Hell,

Send your aid unto my spell.

Horned Huntress of the night,

Work my will by magic rite.

By all the powers of land and sea,

As I do say, "so mote it be."

By all the might of Moon and Sun,

As I do will, it shall be done.

Blessed be!

HOMERIC HYMN

To Selené

Ye Muses, skilled in song, tuneful daughters of Zeus, the Son of Cronos, sing of the fair-faced broad-winged Moon. The gleam from her immortal head, revealed in the sky, rolls round the earth, and much beauty ariseth under her burning light. The murky darkness is lighted up from her golden crown, and her beams flood the air, when divine Selené hath bathed her fair body in the ocean, and done on her far-shining robes, and yoking her strong-necked glossy colts driveth swiftly forward her rich-maned teamsters in the mid—month at eventide. Her great orbit is accomplishing, and her beams are brightest in the sky when she is waxing to the full. She is a mark and a sign for men.

With her once the Son of Cronos mingled in the couch of love, and she conceived and bare a daughter, Pandia, who was gifted with surpassing beauty among the gods.

Hail! O Queen, white—armed goddess, divine Selené, fair—haired and gracious! Beginning with thee I shall sing the praises of heroes, whose deeds minstrels, the henchmen of the Muses, celebrate with charming voices.

—*Translated by John Edgar*

JOSEPH CAMPBELL

Night

Dawn, and awakening from this world of dream, must always have been associated with the sun and sunrise. The night fears and night charms are dispelled by light, which has always been experienced as coming from above and as furnishing guidance and orientation. Darkness, then, and weight, the pull of gravity and the dark interior of the earth, of the jungle, or of the deep sea, as well as certain extremely poignant fears and delights, must for millenniums have constituted a firm syndrome of human experience, in contrast to the luminous flight of the world-awakening solar sphere into and through immeasurable heights. Hence a polarity of light and dark, above and below, guidance and loss of bearings, confidence and fears (a polarity that we all know from our own tradition of thought and feeling and can fine matched in many parts of the world) must be reckoned as inevitable in the way of a structuring principle of human thought. It may or may not be fixed within us as an "isomorph"; but, in any case, it is certainly a general and very deeply known experience.

The moon, furthermore, and the spectacle of the night sky, the stars and the Milky Way, have constituted, certainly from the beginning, a source of wonder and profound impression. But there is actually a physical influence of the moon upon the earth and its creatures, its tides and our own interior tides, which has long been consciously recognized as well as subliminally experienced. The coincidence of the menstrual cycle with that of the moon is a physical actuality structuring human life and a curiosity that has been observed with wonder. It is in fact likely that the fundamental notion of a life-structuring relationship between the heavenly world and that of man was derived from the realization, both in experience and in thought, of the force of the lunar cycle. The mystery, also, of the death and resurrection of the moon, as well as of its influence on dogs, wolves and foxes, jackals and coyotes, which try to sing to it: this immortal silver dish of wonder, cruising among the beautiful stars and racing through the clouds, turning waking life itself into a sort of dream, has been a force and presence even more powerful in the shaping of mythology than the sun, by which its light and its world of stars, night sounds, erotic moods, and the magic of dream, are daily quenched.

NORSE MYTH

Nörfi

"There was a giant living in Giantland called Nörfi or Narfi. He had a daughter named Night. She was dark and swarthy, like the family to which she belonged. Her first marriage was with a man called Naglfari, their son was called Auo. Next she was married to Annar, their daughter was called Earth. Last, Delling married her, and he was of the family of the gods. Their son was Day, he was bright and beautiful like his father's side. Then All-father took Night and her son, Day, and gave them two horses and two chariots and put them up in the sky, so that they should ride round the world every twenty-four hours. Night rides first on a horse called Hrímfaxi, and every morning he bedews the earth with the foam from his bit. Day's horse is called Skinfaxi, and the whole earth and sky are illumined by his mane."

Then Gangleri said: "How does he guide the course of the sun and moon?"

High One replied: "There was a man called Mundilfari who had two children. They were so fair and beautiful that he called one of them Moon and the other, a daughter, Sun; he married her to a man called Glen. The gods, however, were angered at his arrogance and took the brother and sister and put them up in the sky. They made Sun drive the horses which drew the chariot of the sun that the gods had made to light the worlds from a spark which flew from Muspell. The horses are called

Árvak and Alsvio. Under the shoulder-blades of the
horses the gods put two bellows to cool them, and in
some poems that is called iron-cold.

Moon governs the journeying of
the moon and decides the time of
its waxing and waning. He took
from earth two children, known as
Bil and Hjúki, as they were coming

away from the spring called Byrgir carrying on their
shoulders the pail called Soeg and the pole Simul. Their
father's name is Viofinn. These children accompany
Moon, as may be seen from earth."

Then Gangleri said: "The sun moves fast and
almost as if she were afraid; she could not travel faster
if she were in fear of her life."

Then High One answered: "It is not surprising
that she goes at a great pace; her pursuer is close

behind her and there is nothing she can do but flee."

Then Gangleri asked: "Who is it that torments her like this?"

High One replied: "There are two wolves, and the one pursuing her who is called Skoll is the one she fears; he will [ultimately] catch her. The other that runs in front of her, however, is called Hati Hróovitnisson, and he wants to catch the moon and will in the end."

*The First Woman and the
Gift of the Moon*

In the beginning was the woman Lilith and the man Adam. They were wife and husband and lived in a garden called Eden. The garden was so green it rested the eyes like a cool cloth. Its fruits were as many as the stars of the sky. Together Lilith and Adam grew to know the plants and animals they lived with and to lie together, quiet and joyful, under the whispering trees.

But one day Adam took an idea into his head. "Lilith," said Adam, "let's think up a name for each of the animals."

"I don't see a need for that, Adam. Seems like we're all just fine here without names," said Lilith.

But Adam liked his new idea, and he began to spend whole days picking just the right sound for each creature. All day he paced and thought and named animals. Even at dinner he continued his project.

One day Adam said to Lilith, "Lilith, have you ever noticed how big I am? Why, I'm way bigger than you. See?" Adam showed his muscles. "And look how tall I am."

Lilith looked quietly at Adam.

"Lilith, you know what my name is going to be?" said Adam. "King. King. I'm king of this garden."

"I don't like the sound of that, Adam," said Lilith.

"It doesn't really matter if you like the sound, Lilith," said Adam. "I am the biggest and the strongest. So you've got to do what I say."

"You know, Adam, there are other ways to measure bigness than in inches, and other ways to measure strength than in muscles," said Lilith.

"Oh, come on, Lilith," said Adam. "I'm the king, and you're my queen."

"That's not for me, Adam," said Lilith. "The way I see it is that we're all sisters and brothers in this garden. Each of us is as important as the other. Nobody's king and nobody's queen."

Adam didn't listen, so Lilith walked away. The third time Adam started the argument, Lilith took herself out of the garden. Through its gates she went and into the Netherworld. There she sat still and quiet in the dark.

Adam was so furious at Lilith's leave-taking that even when he married the woman Eve and had a family of children, he continued to fume against her. "Snake lover!" he spat. "Not a woman, but a demon!"

"Hush, Adam!" said Eve. "Not in front of the children!"

Lilith alone in the Netherworld grew large. She was going to have a child. Waiting for the child, She gathered a gift to give to the sons and daughters of Adam and Eve. To a girl and a boy sleeping deep in a field She sent the dream of farming.

Soon after that dream was dreamed by the girl and boy, Lilith had Her child. On a black night at the edge of the sea, hanging hard to the dark with Her hands and pushing against it with Her feet, Lilith gave birth to the Moon.

STARHAWK

Moon Meditations and Rituals

WAXING MOON MEDITATION

Ground and center. Visualize a silver crescent moon, curving to the right. She is the power of beginning, of growth and generation. She is wild and untamed, like ideas and plans before they are tempered by reality. She is the blank page, the unplowed field. Feel your own hidden possibilities and latent potentials; your power to begin and grow. See her as a silver-haired girl running freely through the forest under the slim moon. She is Virgin, eternally unpenetrated, belonging to no one but herself. Call her name "Nimuë!" and feel her power within you.

FULL MOON MEDITATION

Ground and center, and visualize a round full moon. She is the Mother, the power of fruition and of all aspects of creativity. She nourishes what the New Moon has begun. See her open arms, her full breasts, her womb burgeoning with life. Feel your own power to nurture, to give, to make manifest what is possible. She is the sexual woman; her pleasure in union is the moving force that sustains all life. Feel the power in your own pleasure, in orgasm. Her color is the red of blood, which is life. Call her name "Mari!" and feel your own ability to love.

WANING MOON MEDITATION

Ground and center. Visualize a waning crescent, curving to the left, surrounded by a black sky. She is the Old Woman, the Crone who has passed menopause, the power of ending, of death. All things must end to fulfill their beginnings. The grain that was planted must be cut down. The blank page must be destroyed, for the work to be written. Life feeds on death—death leads on to life, and in that knowledge lies wisdom. The Crone is the Wise Woman, infinitely old. Feel your own age, the wisdom of evolution stored in every cell of your body. Know your own power to end, to lose as well as gain, to destroy what is stagnant and decayed. See the Crone cloaked in black under the waning moon; call her name "Anu!" and feel her power in your own death.

WAXING MOON RITUAL

(To be performed after the first visible crescent has appeared.)

On the alter, place a bowl of seeds. Fill the central cauldron with earth, and place a candle in the center.

When the coven gathers, begin with a breathing meditation. A Priestess says,

"This is the time of beginning, the seed time of creation, the awakening after sleep. Now the moon emerges, a crescent out of the dark; the Birthgiver returns from Death. The tide turns; all is transformed. Tonight we are touched by the Maiden who yields to all and yet is penetrated by none. She changes everything She touches; may She open us to change and growth. Merry meet."

Purify, cast the circle, and invoke the Goddess and God.

A covener chosen to act as Seed Priestess takes the bowl of grain from the alter, saying,

"Blessed be, creature of earth, moon seed of change,

bright beginning of a new circle of time. Power to start, power to grow, power to make new be in this seed. Blessed be."

Going sunwise around the circle, she offers the bowl to each person, asking, "What will you plant with the moon?" Each person replies with what she plans to begin, or hopes will grow, in the month to come. "The blessing of the new moon be upon it," the Priestess answers.

Each person visualizes a clear image of what they want to grow, charging the seeds with the image. One by one, they plant the seeds in the earth in the central cauldron.

Together, they raise a Cone of Power to charge the seeds and earth with energy, and empower the projects they represent. The Cone is grounded into the cauldron.

Trance work or scrying may focus on clarity of vision for the projects now begun.

Feast, and open the circle.

FULL MOON RITUAL

(To be performed on the eve of the Full Moon.)

The circle gathers, does a breathing meditation, and a Priestess says,

"This is the time of fullness, the flood tide of power, when the Lady in full circle of brightness rides across the night sky, arising with the coming of dark. This is the time of the bearing of fruits, of change realized. The Great Mother, Nurturer of the world, which is Herself, pours out her love and gifts in abundance. The Hunter draws near to the Brilliant One, She who awakens yearning in the heart and who is the end of desire. We who look on her shining face are filled with love. Merry meet."

Purify, cast the circle, and invoke the Goddess and God.

One covener moves into the center of the circle, and speaks her name. The others repeat it, and chant it, raising a Cone of Power as they touch her, earthing it into her and filling her with the power and light of the moon. She returns to the circle, and another covener takes her place, until each in turn has been the focus of the power. While chanting, other coveners come to recognize that each individual is, in truth, Goddess/God.

A final Cone can be raised for the coven as a whole. Earth the power, trance or scry, then feast and open the circle.

Dark Moon Ritual

(To be performed on the waning moon. A gazing crystal or scrying bowl should be placed in the center of the circle.)

Gather, and meditate on a group breath. A Priestess says,

"This is the ending before the beginning, the death before new life. Now on the ebb tide the secrets of the shoreline are uncovered by the retreating waves. The moon is hidden, but the faintest of stars are revealed and those who have eyes to see may read the fates and know the mysteries. The Goddess, whose name cannot be spoken, naked enters the Kingdom of Death. In the most vast silence and stillness, all is possible. We meet in the time of the Crone, to touch the deep power of the dark."

Purify and cast the circle, but do not light the alter candle. Invoke the Goddess and God.

The leader begins an *antiphon* chant: a repeated bass line, with spontaneous lines interjected between.

Leader: "She lies under all, She covers all."

All: "She lies under all, She covers all." (Repeat several times.)

Covener: "She is the teacher of mysteries."

All: "She lies under all, She covers all."

Covener: "She is the motion behind form."

All: "She lies under all, She covers all."

Covener: (Improvised line)

All: "She lies under all, She covers all."

Continue as long as there are energy and inspiration. (This type of chanting requires sensitivity and openness, both to personal inspiration and to others. While at first there may be some hesitations, silences, and collisions, in a cohesive group it will soon flow naturally. It is a powerful way of opening the inner voice.)

Build into a wordless power chant, and earth the cone into the scrying bowl or gazing crystal. Scry together, sharing what you see.

Feast, and open the circle.

CHINESE LEGEND

Heng O,
The Moon Lady

For days, in every court inside the bright red gate of the Lings, there had been comings and goings quite out of the ordinary. In the Garden of Sweet Smells blue-clad workmen were planting in pots new flowers just coming into bloom. The maid servants were putting the houses in order under the watchful eyes of their mistresses. Treasures that had not been taken out of the chests since this time last year were being arranged on tables in the reception hall, where guests might inspect them.

The kitchen was perhaps the busiest of all the little low buildings that stood round the courtyards. There the men cooks and the younger women of the Ling family were working from morning till night, making little round cakes stuffed with almonds and orange peel, melon seeds and sugar, and other good things. They were decorating these cakes with tiny rabbits and toads and pagodas made of sugar. Besides, they were preparing other delicious dishes which they always ate in their celebration of the Moon Lady's birthday on the Fifteenth Day of the Eighth Moon.

The Old Mistress herself, with Fu, the number one servant, and her maid, Huang Ying, spent the days going from one court the other, directing the work of preparing for the feast that was about to take place. Ah Shung and Yu Lang followed her like a shadow. They could hardly wait for the Moon Lady's birthday party to begin. Each time they saw packages brought in through the bright red gate they whispered to each other, "Perhaps it is a pagoda or a moon rabbit for us." Their old nurse, Wang Lai, had taken them to the fair in the temple grounds, where they had seen the toy sellers with their trays of painted clay rabbits and gay-colored toy pagodas.

The Moon Lady's birthday table was set out in the open Courtyard of Politeness. It was covered with a red cloth and laid with five plates filled with fruits as round as the round moon itself. There were apples and peaches, pomegranates and grapes. A pyramid of the little moon-cakes rose high into the air. Candles in pairs and urns filled with incense-sticks stood here and there.

The children were charmed with the splendid clay pagoda which stood in the center to represent the palace of the Moon Lady. Inside it a burning candle sent light shining through each tiny paper windowpane, just as lights shone from the houses round the courtyard. But the boys and girls were even more interested in the tall clay Moon Rabbit in his mandarin's gown, standing up on his long hind legs just like a man. Ah Shung had made a little bundle of bean stalks, the Moon Rabbit's favorite food, and Yu Lang had been allowed to place it herself at the feet of the statue. Near the birthday table, on the courtyard wall, there was a bright printed poster that showed the Moon Rabbit under his cinnamon tree, pounding the pill-of-long-life in his little bowl.

"Heng O, the Moon Lady, comes at last," the Old Old One said to her family as they stood together out in the courtyard. "How she lights up the sky! The moon is larger tonight than at any time of the year."

Everyone watched the round silver disk come slowly out from its hiding place behind the big willow tree. The children gazed at it in wonder. They thought they could trace the outline of the Moon Rabbit upon its bright face, and sometimes they thought they could also find a toad or the Moon Lady, Heng O, herself. Tonight Yu Lang imagined that she could see an open door in the moon, for she had been taught to believe that each year on her birthday the Moon Lady left her shining palace and came down to earth.

The Old Old One led the procession to the birthday table which they had spread in honor of the Moon Lady. She knelt on the stones of the courtyard before it and swayed back and forth in a respectful kowtow. At the same time she said this little prayer to the Queen of the Night:

◗

"O Light One,
O Bright One,
O Wheel of Ice,
O Mirror Bright
We bow tonight,
Bless thou our rice!"

Ah Shung's older sister played sweet tunes on her four-
stringed lute while the Ling family waited, to allow time
for the Moon Lady and the Moon Rabbit to partake of the
good things which they had spread out for them. When
the feasting was over, they sat for a time out in the moonlight. It was the end of summer and in the fields beyond
the city the yellow grain was being cut. But the air was
still warm, and sweet smells were wafted across the
courtyards by the soft night breeze.

"Tonight I must tell you how the lovely Heng O flew
up to the Moon, and how the Moon Rabbit came to be,"
the Old Old One said as she gathered her grandchildren
about her. "It was long, long ago in the time when the
Emperors of China came from the family of Shia. One
day as the Son of Heaven rode forth from the palace in his
yellow sedan chair he saw upon the highway a man with
long arrows and a huge red bow in his hands. The

emperor had never seen another bow like it, and he stopped to examine it.

" 'I am Hou Ye, the bowman,' the man replied to his question. 'With my red bow I shoot arrows from one side of the world to the other. And swift as their flight, I ride on the winds. I am lighter than air because I eat only flowers.' The Emperor was astonished. He hardly believed these words of Hou Ye.

" 'Do you see yonder pine tree on the top of that mountain, O Bowman?' he asked, pointing to a high peak that rose clear and sharp against the blue sky. "If you can indeed shoot from one side of the world to the other, send an arrow through its branches. If you can do that, we shall give you the post of Imperial Archer.'

"The bowman took aim. He bent his red bow, and, straight as a bird flies, his arrow sped to the pine tree on the top of the far mountain. At once the bowman jumped upon a passing wind and flew off to fetch it back to the chair of the Son of Heaven.

"The Emperor kept his promise. He made Hou Ye Imperial Archer, and again and again he called upon him to aim his red bow at some enemy. When a wicked serpent or a tiger did harm to a village, Hou Ye was sent forth to kill him. When the Heavenly Dog tried to eat up the moons, Hou Ye shot an arrow into the sky to drive him away. When the rains did not fall, he would shoot his sharp arrows into the clouds to remind the sky dragons that water was needed.

"One year there came a terrible flood. The rivers spilled out over the fields. People were drowned. Houses and animals were carried away. Sadness filled the land. The Emperor ordered Hou Ye to take his magic bow and seek out Ho Po, the great God of the Waters, who was causing the flood. Quickly the archer mounted the wind and soon found the water spirit. He shot his swift arrows and he wounded Ho Po so that he flew away and never returned to do evil again. Immediately the waters flowed back into the rivers. The country was saved.

"Now, my children, the water spirit had a beautiful sister whose name was Heng O. Hou Ye saw her standing beside her brother, Ho Po, but she was so fair to look upon that he could not bring himself to wound her. When he bent his red bow he was careful to aim his arrow at her thick raven-black hair which she wore in a coil high on her head. The water spirit's sister was so grateful to him for saving her life that she gladly consented to become his wife.

"Not long after, a dreadful thing happened. In the sky there appeared not one sun but ten. Ten round burning disks sent their fierce rays down on the earth. Leaves died on their branches. Grass blades burned to a crisp. No grain could grow. In the terrible heat the water dried up in the wells and the streams. Quickly the Emperor called for Hou Ye.

" 'O Archer,' he said, 'save us as you have saved us before! The soothsayers declare that in each of those suns there lives a golden raven upon whose life the sun's heat and light depends. Take your red bow and shoot the gold ravens! Shoot quickly, O Archer, or we shall all die.'

"Hou Ye drew back his bow. He turned it up toward the sky. Zing-ng-ng! went his arrow as it flew straight and sure to the first of the blazing suns. And before you could finish that moon-cake in your hand, Ah Shung, that sun was gone out of the sky. Zing-ng-ng! A second arrow sped upward to find the second sun. And that ball of fire also was gone. Three, four, five, six, seven, eight, nine sun ravens were killed by the arrows of Hou Ye.

"The archer was just taking aim at the tenth when a

voice came from the clouds. 'Hold, Archer,' it said, 'listen to the Sun God. Leave one sun in the sky so that the earth may be lighted. Without its brightness and warmth no one could live. Take care how you shoot!' So Hou Ye stayed with his hand and the tenth sun still shines, high up there in the heavens.

"The fame of his deed spread far and wide over the earth. It reached the palace of the Empress of the West on the Kun Lun Mountains, and she sent a swift whirlwind to bring Hou Ye before her. With her own hand she put into his a precious pill-of-long-life.

" 'When you swallow this, Mighty Archer,' she said, 'you shall be carried to the heavens, where you will live forever. But do not swallow it now. The time is not ready. For twelve months you must prepare yourself. Hide the pill away. Keep it a secret until the hour comes for you to fly away to the sky.'

"When Hou Ye returned home he followed the advice of the Lady of Kun Lun. He hid the pill-of-long-life carefully up under the roof, and he said never a word about it to anyone, not even to his dear wife, the lovely Heng O.

"It was not long after that the Emperor sent his Imperial Archer on a journey to the south, to fight with a strange man who had round popping eyes and a single sharp tooth from which he got his name, 'Chisel Tooth.'

"While her husband was away Heng O found the time long. One day, as she was going here and there through the house, she saw a bright light high up under the roof. Sweet perfume filled the air. She easily found that the light and the perfume came from the pearly white pill-of-long-life which Hou Ye had hidden. She put the pill into her mouth and, as soon as she had swallowed it, she felt light as a kite and she found she could fly like a bird.

"When her husband returned from killing old Chisel Tooth, he discovered that his precious pill-of-long-life had disappeared, and he sought out Heng O to ask what had become of it. In fear of his anger, she flew out of the window and up to the sky, where she hid in the moon. Hardly had she landed than a fit of coughing seized her, and out of her mouth flew the shell of the pill, which straightway became a rabbit of purest white jade. You can see the Jade Rabbit now on the shining moon disk there above us. Some say Heng O was punished for stealing the pill-of-long-life. They declare she was turned into a toad. But I like to think she is still a fair lady.

"You can imagine that at first Hou Ye was cross," the Old Old One continued. "He mounted a swift wind and rode this way and that way, seeking his wife. The Empress of Kun Lun took pity upon him when he sought her aid. 'Do not fret, Archer,' she said. 'You shall dwell in the sun and you, too shall life forever.' And she gave him a magic cake to eat, in order that he should be able to withstand the fierce heat in his new palace.

"Yet another gift Hou Ye received from the Empress of Kun Lun, a golden bird with a red comb standing high on his head. 'You have been told how to make the sun rise,' said the Empress, 'but how should you know when the hour has come? This golden bird with the red comb will wake you each morning.' And that golden bird which Hou Ye took with him to his palace must have been the ancestor of the roosters in our stable yard that wake us from our sleep each day when the skies first see the sun.

"In his sun palace Hou Ye felt more kindly toward his wife, Heng O. With a charm which the Western Empress had given him, he made his way to the moon to tell her he had forgiven her. He found the moon a sad empty place, ice cold, and with no plants but the cinnamon tree under which the Jade Rabbit stood mixing the pill-of-long-life in his little stone bowl.

"Hou Ye built for his wife her beautiful palace in the moon, and he arranged to visit her there. It is when he comes to see her on the night of the fifteenth of every month that she is largest and fullest. When he goes away she grows paler and paler, and she does not grow bright again until it is time for his visit once more."

"Does Heng O truly come down to earth tonight, Lao Lao?" Yu Lang asked when the old woman ended her story of the Moon Lady.

"I have heard that she does, Precious Pearl," said Grandmother Ling. "They say she goes everywhere and that she listens to the wishes of those who do her honor. But take care, little Yu Lang! If you utter a wish, be sure to speak clearly. There is a story about an old woman who lived long, long ago and who once saw the Moon Lady.

When the Queen of the Night appeared before her, the old woman was so dazzled by her bright beauty that she could not speak a word. Heng O asked what she wished, but the woman was silent. At last she pulled herself together enough to move her trembling hand up and down the lower part of her face. By so doing she meant to show the Moon Lady that she wished only for rice to put into her mouth.

" 'Well, it seems very strange, but if that is what you want you shall have it,' the Moon Lady promised. You see, Heng O had quite misunderstood the old woman's meaning. This was clear the next morning, for there was no more rice than before in the old woman's eating bowl. But when she raised her hand to her mouth she found to her dismay that the Moon Lady had covered her face with gray whiskers. And she had to wait a year, until Heng O's next birthday, before she could wish her beard off again."

—*Translated by Frances Carpenter*

ANCIENT MYTH

Endymion and Selene

For, one calm, clear night Selene looked down upon the beautiful Endymion, who fed his flock on Mount Latmos, and saw him sleeping. The heart of the goddess was unquestionably warmed by his surpassing beauty. She came down to him; she kissed him; she watched over him while he slept. She visited him again and again. But her secret could not long be hidden from the company of Olympus. For more and more frequently she was absent from her station in the sky, and toward morning she was ever paler and more weary

with her watching. When, finally, her love was discovered, Jupiter gave Endymion, who had been thus hon-
ored, a choice between death in any manner that was
preferable, or perpetual youth united with perpetual
sleep. Endymion chose the latter. He still sleeps in his
Carian cave, and still the mistress of the moon slips
from her nocturnal course to visit him. She takes care,
too, that his fortunes shall not suffer from his inactive
life: she yields his flock increase, and guards his sheep
and lambs from beasts of prey.

BEN JONSON

Hymn to Diana

Queen and huntress, chaste and fair,
  Now the sun is laid to sleep,
Seated in thy silver chair,
State in wonted manner keep:
    Hesperus entreats thy light,
    Goddess excellently bright.

Earth, let not thy envious shade
Dare itself to interpose;
Cynthia's shining orb was made

Heaven to clear when day did close:

> Bless us then with wishèd sight,
>
> Goddess excellently bright.

Lay thy bow of pearl apart,
And thy crystal-shining quiver;
Give unto the flying hart
Space to breathe,
how short
soever:

Though that
mak'st a day
of night,

Goddess
excellently bright.

SANTERÍA
FERTILITY RITES

A pomegranate is bought in the name of Yemayá, the beautiful Yoruba moon goddess. She is the patroness of motherhood and it is usually wise to enlist her aid in matters of fertility.

The pomegranate is cut in halves, which are both covered with honey. A piece of paper with the name of the petitioner is placed between the two halves of the pomegranate, which are then put back together again. Yemayá is then invoked and asked that in the same way the pomegranate is rich in health and seeds, so will the petitioner be healthy and fruitful. A blue candle is burned in Yemayá's honor every day for a month, starting with the first day of the menstruation cycle. It is not uncommon that women making this offer to this lovely goddess become pregnant during this month.

TESS
GALLAGHER

Moon Crossing Bridge

If I stand a long time by the river
when the moon is high
don't mistake my attention
for the merely aesthetic, though
that saves in daylight.
Only what we once called worship
has feet light enough to carry
the living on that span of brightness.
And who's to say I didn't cross

just because I used the bridge in its witnessing,

to let the water stay the water

and the incongruities of the moon to chart

the joining I was certain of.

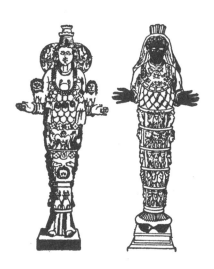

PRE-HELLENIC MYTH

*The Triad of
the Moon*

When the moon appeared as a slender crescent, delicate and fine but firm in the promise of growth, Artemis roamed the untouched forests of Arcadia. The Goddess lived with Her nymphs amid the thick, wild growth where animals joined freely in Her games and dances. She loved new life. Whether at play or at rest, Artemis was ever alert for the rising moans of a mother giving birth. The wind brought to Her long, low sighs and staccato songs of pain expelled. If the mother was an animal, lying alone in a hidden cave or a sheltered pile of leaves, Artemis rushed deftly through the woods to her side. She brought leaves of Her wild artemisia for the animal to eat and spoke softly in the mother's own sounds. The Goddess gently stroked the bulging womb until the wet, squirming bodies emerged. She fondled each one and placed them under Her protection: *Within these forests no harm will touch the children of Artemis.* If the mother was a human, the Goddess appeared instantly at her side bringing artemisia for a potent tea. She wiped the woman's brow and massaged her womb with delicacy and patience, even though She knew the result would be only a meager litter of one or sometimes two. Still, Artemis always appeared to a mother who called and always rejoiced with her at the moment of birth. The other mortals present would come forward for a look, asking, "How is the new one? Who is the new one?" Then

Artemis would smile at the new One and whisper to the mother: *You may both enter My forests without fear and join Me on any night lit by the waxing moon.*

The joining began when the moon was new and continued each night with more and more of Her animals and humans coming to dance with Artemis. On the evening before the full moon Her sacred grove was filled with celebrants. They encircled a large tree that stood apart from the others, its smooth bark and leaves seeming silver in the moonlight. Artemis moved toward the tree and silence followed, but for Her doves cooing softly in the boughs overhead. The Goddess

crouched as the Great She-Bear She once had been and touched the earth. From the roots, up the trunk, along the branches to the leaves She drew her hands. Again. And again. With each pass She brought forth new life: pale blossoms unfolding and falling away, tiny globes of fruit shining among the branches, and finally ripe, glowing fruit hanging heavily from the sacred boughs. Artemis gathered the fruit and fed Her animals, Her mortals, Her nymphs, and Herself. The dance began.

The animals were drawn to the tree. They rolled over its roots and encircled the trunk. In a larger ring the dancers raised their arms, turning slowly, and felt currents of energy rising from the earth through their legs, turning, through their trunks, turning faster, through their arms, turning, out their fingers, turning, turning, to their heads, whirling, racing, flying. Sparks of energy flew from their fingertips, lacing the air with traces of clear blue light. They joined hands,

joined arms, merged bodies into a circle of unbroken current that carried them effortlessly. Artemis appeared large
before them standing straight against the tree, Her spine its
trunk, Her arms its boughs. Her body pulsed with life, its
rhythms echoed by the silvered tree, the animals at Her feet,
the dancers, the grass, the plants, the grove. Every particle
of the forest quivered with Her energy. Artemis the nurturer, protector, Goddess of the swelling moon. Artemis!
She began to merge with the sacred tree, while the circle of
dancers spun around Her. They threw back their heads and
saw the shimmering boughs rush by. When Artemis was
one with the moon tree, the circle broke. Dancers went
whirling through the grove, falling exhausted on the mossy
forest floor.

Lying there on the earth, still breathing in rhythm
with the earth, they stared up at the constant dancers in the
heavens. Through the stars Selene was cutting a path with

Her chariot. The winged Goddess drove a pair of oxen, whose horns echoed the crescent moon on Her own crown. Behind Her Selene pulled the full moon across the sky. She rose from the ocean and climbed steadily with the enormous disc to Her zenith, where it gradually shrank in size and She easily glided downward to the ocean once again. When Selene crossed the heavens, Her light flooded the earth, filtering down through the hidden cracks and crevices in the nature of mortal beings. They marked Her passage, joined in small groups to celebrate, and treated with awe those touched by Her magic.

But when the moon slipped away, shrinking gracefully into its own death, there were no festivities. The nights grew blacker and the mortals guarded themselves against visiting spirits from the underworld. Hoards of ghosts led by Hecate and Her baying hounds of hell roamed the earth on moonless nights. Yet She protected those mortals who purified themselves in Her name. With faces averted they offered Her ritual suppers at lonely crossroads, the gathering place of spirits. When Hecate's rites were observed the black nights passed silently one into another. But if the Goddess was defied, She unleashed the power of Her wrath and swept over the earth, bringing storms and destruction. Animals howled in fright, while Her ghosts stalked freely.

Hecate's disturbances were fierce, yet not all of the mortals feared them. Some longed to join Her. In the dark of the moon small covens awaited Her near drooping willow trees. She appeared suddenly before them with Her torch and Her hounds. A nest of snakes writhed in Her hair, sometimes shedding, sometimes renewing. Until the new moon slit the sky, Hecate shared clues to Her secrets. Those who believed understood. They saw that form was not fixed, watched human become animal become tree become human. They witnessed the power of Her favored herbs: black poppy, smilax, mandragora, aconite. Awesome were Her skills but always Hecate taught the same lesson: *Without death there is no life.*

APULEIUS

Isis

About the first watch of the night, when as I had slept my first sleep, I awaked with sudden fear, and saw the moon shining bright as when she is at the full, and seeming as though she leaped out of the sea. Then I thought with myself that this was the most secret time, when that goddess had most puissance and force, considering that all human things be governed by her providence; and that not only all beasts private and tame, wild and savage, be made strong by the governance of her light and godhead, but also things inanimate and

without life; and I considered that all bodies in the heavens, the earth, and the seas be by her increasing motions
increased, and by her diminishing motions diminished:
then as weary of all my cruel fortune and calamity, I
found good hope and sovereign remedy, though it were
very late, to be delivered of all my misery, by invocation and prayer to the excellent beauty of this powerful
goddess. Wherefore shaking off my drowsy sleep I
arose with a joyful face, and moved by a great affection
to purify myself, I plunged my head seven times into the
water of the sea; which number of seven is convenable
and agreeable to holy and divine things, as the worthy
and sage philosopher Pythagoras hath declared. Then
very lively and joyfully, though with a weeping counte-
nance, I made this oration to the puissant goddess:

"O blessed queen of heaven, whether Thou be
the Dame Ceres which art the original and motherly

nurse of all fruitful things in the earth, who, after the finding of Thy daughter Proserpine, through the great joy which Thou didst presently conceive, didst utterly take away and abolish the food of them of old time, the acorn, and madest the barren and unfruitful ground of Eleusis to be ploughed and sown, and now givest men a more better and milder food; or whether Thou be the celestial Venus, who, in the beginning of the world, didst couple together male and female with an engendered love, and didst so make an eternal propagation of human kind, being now worshipped within the temples of the Isle Paphos; or whether Thou be the sister of the god Phoebus, who hast saved so many people by lightening and lessening with thy medicines the pangs of travail and art now adored at the sacred places of Ephesus; or whether Thou be called terrible Proserpine, by reason of the deadly howlings which Thou yieldest, that hast power with triple face to stop and put away the invasion of hags and ghosts which appear unto men, and to keep them down in the closures of the Earth, which dost wander in sundry groves and art worshipped in divers manners; Thou, which dost luminate all the cities of the earth by Thy feminine light; Thou, which nourishest all the seeds of the world by Thy damp heat, giving Thy changing light according to the wanderings, near or far, of the sun: by whatsoever name or fashion or shape it is lawful to call upon Thee, I pray Thee to end in my great travail and misery and raise up my fallen hopes, and deliver me from the wretched fortune which so long time pursued me. Grant peace and rest, if it please Thee, to my adversities, for I have endured enough labour and peril. Remove from me the hateful shape of mine ass, and render me to my kindred and to mine own self Lucius:

and if I have offended in any point Thy divine majesty, let me rather die if I may not live."

When I had ended this oration, discovering my plaints to the goddess, I fortuned to fall again asleep upon that same bed; and by and by (for mine eyes were but newly closed) appeared to me from the midst of the sea a divine and venerable face, worshipped even of the gods themselves. Then, by little and little, I seemed to see the whole figure of her body, bright and mounting out of the sea and standing before me: wherefore I purpose to describe her divine semblance, if the poverty of my human speech will suffer me, or her divine power give me a power of eloquence rich enough to express it. First she had a great abundance of hair, flowing and curling, dispersed and scattered about her divine neck; on the crown of her head she bare many garlands interlaced with flowers, and in the middle of her forehead was a plain circlet in fashion of a mirror, or rather resembling the moon by the light that it gave forth; and this was borne up on either side by serpents that seemed to rise from the furrows of the earth, and above it were blades of corn set out. Her vestment was of finest linen yielding divers colours, somewhere white and shining, somewhere yellow like the crocus flower, somewhere rosy red, somewhere flaming; and (which troubled my sight and spirit sore) her cloak was utterly dark and obscure covered with shining black, and being wrapped round her from under her left arm to her right shoulder in a manner of a shield, part of it fell down, pleated in most subtle fashion, to the skirts of her garment so that the welts appeared comely. Here and there upon the edge thereof and throughout its surface the stars glimpsed, and in the middle of them was placed the moon in mid-month, which shone like a flame of fire; and round about the whole length of the border of that goodly robe was a crown or garland wreathing unbroken, made with all flowers and all fruits. Things quite diverse did she bear: for in her right hand she had a timbrel of brass, a flat piece of metal curved in the manner of a girdle, wherein passed not many rods through the periphery of it; and when with her arm she moved these triple chords, they gave forth a shrill and clear sound. In her left hand she bare a cup of gold like unto a boat, upon the handle whereof, in the upper part which is best seen, an asp lifted up his head with a wide-swelling throat. Her odoriferous feet were covered with shoes interlaced and wrought with victorious palm. Thus the divine shape, breathing out the pleasant spice of fertile Arabia, disdained not with her holy voice to utter these words unto me:

"Behold, Lucius, I am come; thy weeping and prayer hath moved me to succour thee. I am she that is the natural mother of all things, mistress and governess of all the elements, the initial progeny of worlds, chief of the powers divine, queen of all that are in hell, the principal of them that dwell in heaven, manifested alone and under one form of all the gods and goddesses. At my will the planets of the sky, the wholesome winds of the seas, and the lamentable silences of hell be disposed; my name, my divinity is adored throughout all the world, in divers manners, in variable customs, and by many names. For the Phrygians that are the first of all men call me the Mother of the gods at Pessinus; the Athenians, which are sprung from their own soil, Cecropian Minerva; the Cyprians, which are girt about by the sea, Paphian Venus; the Cretans which bear arrows, Dictynnian Diana; the Sicilians, which speak three tongues, infernal Proserpine; the Eleusians their ancient goddess Ceres; some Juno, other Bellona, other Hecate, other Rhamnusia, and principally both sort of the Ethiopians which dwell in the Orient and are enlightened by the morning rays of the sun, and the Egyptians, which are excellent in all kind of ancient doctrine, and by their proper ceremonies accustom to worship me, do call me by my true name, Queen Isis. Behold I am come to take pity of thy fortune and tribulation; behold I am present to favour and aid thee; leave off thy weeping and lamentation, put away all thy sorrow, for behold the healthful day which is ordained by my providence. Therefore be ready and attentive to my commandment; the day which shall come after this night is dedicate to my service by an eternal religion; my priests and ministers do accustom, after the wintry and stormy tempests of the sea be ceased and the billows of his waves are still, to offer in my name a new ship, as a first-fruit of their navigation; and for this must thou wait, and not profane or despise the sacrifice in any wise. For the great priest shall carry this day following in procession, by my exhortation, a garland of roses next to the timbrel of his right hand; delay not, but, trusting to my will, follow that my procession passing amongst the crowd of the people, and when thou comest to the priest, make as though thou wouldst kiss his hand, but snatch at the roses and thereby put away the skin and shape of an ass, which kind of beast I have long time abhorred and despised. But above all things beware thou doubt not nor fear of any of those my things as hard and difficult to be brought to pass; for in this same hour that I am come to thee, I am present there also, and I command the priest by a vision what he shall do, as here followeth: and all the people by my commandment shall be compelled to give thee place and say nothing. Moreover, think not that amongst so fair and joyful ceremonies, and in so good company, that any person shall abhor thy ill-favoured and deformed figure, or that any man shall be so hardy as to blame and reprove thy sudden restoration to human shape, whereby they should gather or conceive any sinister opinion of thee; and know thou this of certainty, that the residue of thy life until the hour of death shall be bound and subject to me; and think it not an injury to be always serviceable towards me whilst though shalt live, since as by my mean and benefit thou shalt return again to be a man. Thou shalt live blessed in this world, thou shalt live glorious by my guide and protection, and when after thine allotted space of life thou descendest to hell, there thou shalt see me in that subterranean firmament shining (as thou seest me now) in the darkness of Acheron, and reigning in the deep profundity of Styx, and thou shalt worship me as one that hath been favorable to thee. And if I perceive that thou art obedient to my commandment and addict to my religion, meriting by thy constant chastity my divine grace, know thou that I alone may prolong thy days above the time that the fates have appointed and ordained."

When the invincible goddess had spoken these words and ended her holy oracle, she vanished away. By and by when I awaked, I arose, having the members of my body mixed with fear, joy, and heavy sweat, and marvelled at the clear presence of the puissant goddess, and when I had sprinkled myself with the water of the sea, I recounted orderly her admonitions and divine commandments. Soon after the darkness was chased away and the clear and golden sun arose, when behold, I saw the streets replenished with people, going in a religious sort, and in great triumph. All things seemed that day to be joyful, as well all manner of beasts and the very houses, as also even the day itself seemed to rejoice.

—Translated by W. Adlington

EMILY DICKINSON

The Moon Was But a Chin of Gold

The Moon was but a Chin of Gold
A Night or two ago—
And now she turns Her perfect Face
Upon the World below—

Her Forehead is of Amplest Blonde—
Her Cheek—a Beryl hewn—
Her Eye unto the Summer Dew
The likest I have known—

Her Lips of Amber never part—
But what must be the smile
Upon Her Friend she could confer
Were such Her Silver Will—

And what a privilege to be
But the remotest Star—
For Certainty She take Her Way
Beside Your Palace Door—

Her Bonnet is the Firmament—
The Universe—Her Shoe—
The Stars—the Trinkets at Her Belt—
Her Dimities—of Blue—

THE BOOK OF REVELATION

Chapter 12,

Verses 1—6

And a great portent appeared in heaven, a woman clothed with the sun, with the moon under her feet, and on her head a crown of twelve stars; she was with child and she cried out in her pangs of birth, in anguish for delivery. And another portent appeared in heaven; behold, a great red dragon, with seven heads and ten horns, and seven diadems upon his heads. His tail swept down a third of the stars of heaven, and cast them to earth. And the dragon stood before the woman who was about to bear a child, that he might devour her child when she brought it forth; she brought forth a male child, one who is to rule all the nations with a rod of iron, but her child was caught up to God and to his throne, and the woman fled into the wilderness, where she has a place prepared by God, in which to be nourished for one thousand two hundred and sixty days.

RIG VEDA

To Night

With all her eyes the goddess Night looks forth
    approaching many a spot:
She hath put all her glories on.

Immortal, she hath filled the waste, the goddess hath
    filled height and depth:
She conquers darkness with her light.

The Goddess as she comes hath set Dawn her Sister
    in her place:
And then the darkness vanishes.

So favor us this night, O thou whose pathways we
  have visited
As birds their nest upon the tree.

The villagers have sought their homes, and all that
  walks and all that flies,
Even the falcons fain for prey.

Keep off the she-wolf and the wolf; O Night, keep
  the thief away:
Easy be thou for us to pass.

Clearly hath she come nigh to me who decks the dark

with richest hues:

O Morning, cancel it like debts.

These have I brought to thee like kine [= cattle]. O

Night, thou Child of Heaven, accept

This laud as for a conqueror.

—*Translated by David Smith*

HENRY DAVID THOREAU

Diana Still Hunts

The Hindoos compare the moon to a
saintly being who has reached the last stage
of bodily existence.
Not secondary to the sun, she
        gives us his blaze again,
Void of its flame, and sheds a softer day.
Now through the passing cloud she seems
    to stoop,
Now up the pure cerulean rides sublime.

The whole air whitens with a boundless tide
Of silver radiance, trembling round the world.

Diana still hunts in the New England sky.

In Heaven queen she is among the spheres;
She, mistress—like, makes all things to be pure;
Eternity in her oft change she bears;
She Beauty is; by her the fair endure.

Time wears her not; she doth his chariot guide;
Mortality below her orb is placed;
By her the virtues of the stars down slide;
By her is Virtue's perfect image cast.

Great restorer of antiquity, great en-
chanter. In a mild night when the harvest or

hunter's moon shines full, the houses in our

village, whatever architect they

may have had by day,

acknowledge only Vitruviuses

or a greater than Vitruvius.

And the village is there as well as

the forest.

In such a night let me abroad remain

  remain

Till morning breaks, and all's confused again.

PRINCESS
ENHEDUANNA

*Hymn to the
Goddess Inanna*

Despite the great importance of goddesses in later Hinduism, most of the hymns in the *Rig Veda* are devoted to the male gods who dominate the early pantheon. While goddesses rarely receive ritual offerings, there are a few hymns to various goddesses, though none of them have either the power or the popularity of a god such as Indra. In the main these goddesses are associated with natural phenomena.

The next two hymns (X:127 and VII:77) praise the

sister goddesses, Night and Dawn. Night is perceived to be fearful, so the hymn invokes her protection. Dawn, on the other hand, is considered auspicious and a bringer of riches.

INANNA AND ENLIL

Devastatrix of the lands,

   you are lent wings by the storm.

Beloved of Enlil,

   you fly about in the nation.

You are at the service

   of the decrees of An.

Oh my lady, at the sound of you

   the lands bow down.

When mankind

   comes before you

In fear and trembling

at (your) tempestuous radiance,

They receive from you

their just deserts.

Proffering a song of lamentation,

they weep before you,

They walk toward you along the

path of the house of all the great

sighs.

THE BANISHMENT [OF ENHEDUANNA] FROM UR

Verily I had entered

my holy *gipáru* at your behest,

I, the high priestess,

I, Enheduanna!

I carried the ritual basket,

I intoned the acclaim.

(But now) I am placed in the leper's ward,

I, even I, can no longer live with you!

THE INDICTMENT OF NANNA
[THE MOON GOD]

As for me, my Nanna

takes no heed of me.

He has verily given me over to destruction

in murderous straits.

Ashimbabbar

has not pronounced my judgment.

Had he pronounced it: what is it to me?

Had he not pronounced it: what is it

to me?

(Me) who once sat triumphant

he has driven out of the

sanctuary.

Like a swallow he made me fly

from the window,

my life is consumed.

He made me walk

in the bramble of the

mountain.

He stripped me of the crown

appropriate for the high

priesthood.

He gave me a dagger and

sword—

"it becomes you," he said

to me.

THE APPEAL TO INANNA

Most precious lady,

  beloved of An,

Your holy heart is lofty,

  may it be assuaged on my behalf!

Beloved bride

  of Ushumgalanna,

You are the senior queen

  of the heavenly foundations and zenith.

The Anunna

  have submitted to you.

From birth on

  you were the "junior" queen.

How supreme you are over the great gods,

  the Anunna!

The Anunna kiss the ground with their
   lips (in obeisance) to you.

(But) my own sentence is not
   concluded a hostile judgment
   appears before my eyes as my
   judgment.
(My) hands are no longer folded
   on the ritual couch,
I may no longer reveal
   the pronouncements of Ningal
   to man.

(Yet) I am the brilliant
   high priestess of Nanna,
Oh my queen beloved of An,
   may your heart take pity on me!

THE EXALTATION OF INANNA

That one has not recited as a "Known!

  Be it known!" of Nanna,

    that one has recited as a " 'Tis Thine!":

"That you are lofty as Heaven—

  be it known!

That you are broad as the earth—

  be it known!

That you devastate the rebellious land—

  be it known!

That you roar at the land—

  be it known!

That you smite the heads—

  be it known!

That you devour cadavers like a dog—

  be it known!

That your glance is terrible—

   be it known!

That you lift your terrible glance—

   be it known!

That your glance is flashing—

   be it known!

That you are ill-disposed toward the . . .

   be it known!

That you attain victory—

   be it known!"

That one has not recited (this) of Nanna,

   that one has recited it as a " 'Tis Thine!"—

(That,) oh my lady, has made you great,

   you alone are exalted!

Oh my lady beloved of An,

   I have verily recounted your fury!

SYLVIA PLATH

Last Words

I do not want a plain box, I want a sarcophagus
   With tigery stripes, and a face on it
Round as the moon, to stare up.
I want to be looking at them when they come
Picking among the dumb minerals, the roots.
I see them already—the pale, star-distance faces.
Now they are nothing, they are not even babies.
I imagine them without fathers or mothers, like
   the first gods.
They will wonder if I was important.

I should sugar and preserve my days like fruit!

My mirror is clouding over—

A few more breaths, and it will reflect nothing at all.

The flowers and the faces whiten to a sheet.

I do not trust the spirit. It escapes like steam

In dreams, through mouth-hole or eye-hole. I can't

   stop it.

One day it won't come back. Things aren't like that.

They stay, their little particular lusters

Warmed by much handling.

   They almost purr.

When the soles of my feet

   grow cold,

The blue eye of my turquoise

   will comfort me.

Let me have my copper

cooking pots, let my rouge pots

Bloom about me like night flowers, with a good

smell.

They will roll me up in bandages, they will store my

heart

Under my feet in a neat parcel.

I shall hardly know myself. It will be dark,

And the shine of these small things sweeter than the

face of Ishtar.

TARANATHA

*The Goddess
Tara*

Long ago, in an age before which there was nothing else, the Victorious One, the Tathāgata Dundubhisvara came into existence and was known as the
Light of the Various Worlds. The Princess "Moon of
Wisdom" had the highest respect for his teaching, and
for ten million, one hundred thousand years, she made
offerings to this Enlightened One, his attendant Srāvakas
and to countless members of the Sangha of Bodhisattvas.
The offerings she prepared each day were in value
comparable to all the precious things which filled a dis-

tance of twelve yojanas in each of the ten directions, leaving no intermediate spaces unfilled. Finally, after all this she awoke to the first concepts of Bodhi-Mind. At that time some monks said to her, "It is as a result of these, your roots of virtuous actions, that you have come into being in this female form. If you pray that your deeds accord with the teachings, then indeed on that account you will change your form to that of a man, as if befitting." After much discourse she finally replied, "In this life there is no distinction as "male" and "female," neither of "self-identity," a "person" nor any perception (of such), and therefore attachment to ideas of "male" and "female" is quite worthless. Weak-minded worldlings are always deluded by this." And so she vowed, "There are many who wish to gain enlighten-ment in a man's form, and there are but few who wish to work for the welfare of sentient beings in a female form. Therefore may I, in a female body, work for the welfare of beings right until Samsāra has been emptied."

Then she remained in the palace for ten million and one hundred thousand years in a state of meditation, wisely applying her mind to the five sensual pleasures. As a result of this she gained success in the realization that dharmas are non-originating and also perfected the meditation known as "Saving All Sentient Beings," by the power of which, every morning she released ten million and one hundred thousand beings from (the bondage of) their worldly minds. As long as all of them were not fully

instructed in this steadfast course, she would take no nourishment at all. This same policy was followed each evening when she set a like number of beings on the same path. Then her former name was changed and she became known as the Saviouress. Then the Tathāgatha Dundubhisvara prophesies: "As long as you can possibly continue manifesting such supreme Bodhi, you will be exclusively known as 'Goddess Tārā.'"

—Translated by David Templeman

LADY MARY
WORTLEY MONTAGU

A Hymn to
the Moon

Thou silver deity of secret night,
    Direct my footsteps through the
woodland shade;
Thou conscious witness of unknown
    delight,
    The lover's guardian, and the Muses'
    aid!
By thy pale beams I solitary rove,
    To thee my tender grief confide;

Serenely sweet you gild the silent grove,

My friend, my goddess, and my guide.

E'en thee, fair queen,

from thy amazing

height,

The charms of

young Endymion

drew;

Veil'd with the mantle

of concealing night;

With all thy greatness, and thy coldness too.

PERCY BYSSHE SHELLEY

The Cloud

That orbèd maiden, with white fire laden,

    Whom mortals call the Moon,

Glides glimmering o'er my fleece-like floor,

    By the midnight breezes strewn;

And wherever the beat of her unseen feet,

    Which only the angels hear,

May have broken the woof of my tent's thin roof,

    The stars peep behind her and peer;

And I laugh to see them whirl and flee,

Like a swarm of golden bees,

When I widen the rent in my wind-built tent,

Till the calm rivers, lakes and seas,

Like strips of the sky fallen through me on high,

Are each paved with the moon and these.

PRE-HELLENIC MYTH

Hera

On the morning of the new moon, the women of Argos left their homes and walked together to the Stream of the Freeing Water. They bathed and then gathered branches from the nearby lygos bushes, which they laid in a large circular bower. On this ring they sat throughout the day, each seated with the women of her mother's clan. With the blessing of the Goddess, the lygos encouraged the flow of their sacred blood that would complete the cleansing they had begun in the stream. Although the women fasted, their mood was not somber. They talked of their crops, their herds, their children and listened to stories told by the elders. As twilight approached, they began chants and songs that summoned Hera in Her manifestation of the new moon. When Hera appeared as a pale sliver climbing above the horizon, the women responded by lighting a fire in the center of their circle and continued the songs. Gradually Hera drew forth the blood of purification and renewed fertility. Gradually the chanting increased in tempo. Those who had received Hera's gift shared it with the young, the pregnant, and the old women by painting a red crescent moon on their foreheads. All rose, giving praise to the Goddess, and returned in a torchlit procession to their homes.

Hidden in the foothills nearby, the spring called *Kanathos* flowed secretly, silently from the Earth's womb. Each year Hera appeared to the Argive women at the spring. She bathed in the cool water and emerged with Her virginity renewed once again—

One-In-Herself, the Celestial Virgin. The women received the blessing of Hera's grace and crowned one another with wreaths of aster, blossoming with the Goddess' starflowers. They followed Hera to a broad terrace on the side of Mount Euboia, Her sacred ground.

The Goddess looked down onto the plain stretching out before Her. All the people of Argos, all the animals, all the colors of spring had come together for the Sacred Marriage. Hera presided over the joining of the lunar cow and the solar bull. Then She looked out over the assembly and blessed the Argives with unfailing fecundity of field and womb. They celebrated the promise of their survival with dances and feasting. On that day began again the homage to Hera which continued throughout the year.

Every four years the benevolence of the Goddess was celebrated at the feast of the Heraia. At Olympia
Hera watched the footraces run in Her name. The races
were run by girls divided into three age groups to represent the three phases of the moon and the corresponding
three stages of woman's life. The winners were awarded
an olive wreath and the honor of resembling the Goddess
most closely. As Hera crowned the youngest winner, the
girl addressed the crowd: *I am the new moon, swelling with
magic, pure in my maidenhood, ever growing stronger.* The
second winner spoke: *I am the full moon, complete in my
powers, making people with my rhythms, bathing them in light.*
The third said: *I am the waning moon, shrinking into peace,
knowing all that went before, I am the old one.*

MARGE PIERCY

*The moon is
always female*

The moon is always female and so
    I am I although often in this vale

of razorblades I have wished I could

put on and take off my sex like a dress

and why not? Do men wear their sex

always? The priest, the doctor, the teacher

all tell us they come to their professions

neuter as clams and the truth is

when I work I am pure as an angel

tiger and clear is my eye and hot

my brain and silent all the whining

grunting piglets of the appetites.

For we were priests to the goddesses

to whom were fashioned the first alters

of clumsy stone on stone and leaping animal

in the wombdark caves, long before men

put on skirts and masks to scare babies.

For we were healers with herbs and poultices

with our milk and careful fingers

long before they began learning to cut up

the living by making jokes at corpses.

For we were making sounds from our throats

and lips to warn and encourage the

  helpless

young long before schools were built

to teach boys to obey and be bored and kill.

I wake in a strange slack empty bed

of a motel, shaking like dry leaves

the wind rips loose, and in my head

is bound a girl of twelve whose female

organs all but the numb womb are being

cut from her with a knife. Clitoridectomy,

whatever Latin name you call it, in a quarter

of the world girl children are so maimed

and I think of her and I cannot stop.

And I think of her and I cannot stop.

If you are a woman you feel the knife in

the words.

If you are a man, then at age four or else

at twelve you are seized and held down

and your penis is cut off. You are left

your testicles but they are sewed to your

crotch. When your spouse buys you, you
are torn or cut open so that your precious
semen can be siphoned out, but of course
you feel nothing. But pain. But pain.

For the uses of men we have been butchered
and crippled and shut up and carved open
under the moon that swells and shines
and shrinks again into nothingness, pregnant
and then waning toward its little monthly
death. The moon is always female but the sun
is female only in lands where females
are let into the sun to run and climb.

A woman is screaming and I hear her.
A woman is bleeding and I see her
bleeding from the mouth, the womb, the breasts

in a fountain of dark blood of dismal
daily tedious sorrow quite palatable
to the taste of the mighty and taken for granted
that the bread of domesticity be baked
of our flesh, that the hearth be built
of our bones of animals kept for meat and milk,
that we open and lie under and weep.
I want to say over the names of my mothers
like the stones of a path I am climbing
rock by slippery rock into the mists.
Never even at knife point have I wanted
or been willing to be or become a man.
I want only to be myself and free.

I am waiting for the moon to rise. Here
I squat, the whole country with its steel
mills and its coal mines and its prisons

at my back and the continent tilting

up into mountains and torn by shining lakes

all behind me on this scythe of straw,

a sand bar cast on the ocean waves, and I

wait for the moon to rise red and heavy

in my eyes. Chilled, cranky, fearful

in the dark I wait and I am all the time

climbing slippery rocks in a mist while

far below the waves crash in the sea caves;

I am descending a stairway under the groaning

sea while the black waters buffet me

like rockweed to and fro.

I have swum the upper waters leaping

in dolphin's skin for joy equally into the nec-

essary air and the tumult of the powerful wave.

I am entering the chambers I have visited.

I have floated through them sleeping and sleep-
walking and waking, drowning in passion
festooned with green bladderwrack of misery.
I have wandered these chambers in the rock
where the moon freezes the air and all hair
is black or silver. Now I will tell you
what I have learned lying under the moon
naked as women do: now I will tell you
the changes of the high and lower moon.
Out of necessity's hard stones we suck
what water we can and so we have survived,
women born of women. There is knowing
with the teeth as well as knowing with
the tongue and knowing with the fingertips
as well as knowing with words and with all
the fine flickering hungers of the brain.

NAVAJO CREATION MYTH

*Song of the
Sun and Moon*

The first man holds it in his hands,
He holds the sun in his hands.
In the center of the sky, he holds it in his hands.
As he holds it in his hands, it starts upward.

The first woman holds it in her hands,
She holds the moon in her hands.
In the center of the sky, she holds it in her hands.
As she holds it in her hands, it starts upward.

The first man holds it in his hands,

He holds the sun in his hands.

In the center of the sky, he holds it in his hands.

As he holds it in his hands, it
starts downward.

The first woman holds it in
her hands,

She holds the moon in her
hands.

In the center of the sky, she
holds it in her hands.

As she holds it in her hands, it starts downward.

—*Translated by Mary C. Wheelwright*

H . D .

Thetis is the Moon-goddess
and can change her shape,
she is Selene, is Artemis;

she is the Moon, her sphere
is remote, white, near,
is *Leuké*, is marble and snow,

is here; this is Leuké,
a-drift, a shell but held
to its central pole

or its orbit;

this is the white island,

this is the hollow shell,

this is the ship a-drift,

this is the ship at rest,

let me stay here;

is it Death to know

this immaculate purity,

security?

Illustrations

Pages 9, 144 – The Sacred Moon Tree of Chaldea with fruits.

Pages 12, 127 – The Gateway of the Shrine of Paphos. Here the stone resembles the Emblem of Isis, which represents the female genitalia, symbol of womanhood. From the *Symbolical Language of Ancient Art and Religion*, R. Payne Knight, 1892.

Page 15 – This symbol consisting of the crescent moon above three pillars or buds is found on the walls of the catacombs and is entitled "The Kingdom of Heaven."

Pages 28, 37, 97, 109, 114, 136 – Three forms of the Sacred Moon Tree of Assyria, showing the gradual conventionalization till it is a mere stump or pillar. All from *Sur la Culte de Mithra*, Felix Lajard, 1847.

Page 35 – Assyrian Winged Moon, from an Assyrian Cylinder, probably eighteenth dynasty. The moon is shown winged for its flight through the heavens. The god is enthroned in the crescent as in a boat or chariot. Streams of heavenly nectar, or soma, pour down and are caught in goblets below. From *Symbolism on Greek Coins*, Agnes Baldwin Brett, American Numismatic Society, 1916.

Page 37 – The Sacred Moon Tree of Chaldea with trellis and torches.

Page 41 – The Sacred Stone of the Moon Goddess. From *Sur la Culte de Venus*, Felix Lajard, 1837

Pages 45, 132 – The Sacred Moon Tree of Chaldea, enclosed by a trellis.

Pages 48, 49 – Shrine of the Sacred Moon Tree from Minoa, Crete. From *Themis* by Jane Harrison, copyright 1912 by permission of the Cambridge Univ. Press and the Macmillan Co. publishers.

Page 67 – The Sacred Moon Tree of Babylon. This form resembles a lotus. The lower branches bear torches, symbolizing the light of the moon.

Page 73 – The Chariot of the Moon. The Crescent Moon is here shown being drawn in a chariot by goats. The Goddess Cybele in human form is often seen in a similar chariot replacing the lunar crescent. From *Sur la Culte de Mithra*, Felix Lajard, 1847.

Page 75 – The Solar King and Lunar Queen, circa 1600.

Page 77, 135 – Pre-Christian symbols found in Greek churches. The cross and the crescent and the pole and the crescent, probably both related to the moon tree.

Page 79 – Diana, or Artemis, the "many breasted" mother of all living creatures in her dual aspect, the dark and the light. She is "many breasted" to signify her all-nurturing, all-fostering character. Her animal children are grouped upon

her. From *Ancient Pagan and Modern Christian Symbolism*,
Thomas Inman, 1876

Page 82 —Left to right: (a) In this archaic statuette,
Astarte, or Ishtar, is shown crowned with the crescent moon.
She is "many breasted" and stands upon a base decorated with
crescents. From *Religions de l'Antiquité*, Georg Frederic
Creuzer, 1825. (b) Selene, the Moon Goddess of Greece,
stands on the arc of the moon which rests like a boat on the
waters. She is crowned with the crescent and holds back the
"peblum" or tent of the sky so as to reveal herself. From *A
New System or Analysis of Ancient Mythology*, Jacob Bryant,
1774. (c) Pre-Christian Virgin and Child found in Greek
churches.

Page 86 — The Moon Deity is here represented by a
snake-encoiled tree and two stones. In front is a hound and a
shell, emblem of the feminine principle. From *A New System or
Analysis of Ancient Mythology*, Jacob Bryant, 1774.

Page 101 — The symbol of the crescent moon.

Page 103 — This picture comes from Ur and dates from
about 2300 to 210 B.C. The moon god is seated in a crescent
boat and is paddling himself across the sky. The Hero is
shown fighting a lion and a unicorn, they are probably the
monsters who threaten to devour the moon. From the British
Museum.

Page 105 – The Moon Barge. This is an Egyptian Moon Boat. It is said to be self-propelled. Within it rests the moon, the crescent holding the full moon within its horns. It is guarded in its journey by the two Eyes of Horus. From *Dawn of Civilization*, G. Maspero, The Appleton-Century Co.

Page 120 – Phoenician Stella, the Moon Deity represented in Triune from. Three stones or pillars of unequal height represent the three phases of the moon. From *Themis*, Jane Harrison, the Cambridge University Press, and the Macmillan Company, 1912.

Page 124 – Left to right: (a) The Sacred Stone of the Moon Goddess, enshrined in her temple. The image is shown as a simple cone or omphalos. From *Religions de l'Antiquité*, Georg F. Creuzer, 1825. (b) The Sacred Stone of the Moon Goddess. The simple stone has an added part like a head. From *Religions de l'Antiquité*, Georg F. Creuzer, 1825.

Page 129 – East of the Sun, A. Lang, 1879.

Page 142 – Hungarian Etching, 1869.

Biographies

Sasha Fenton - Fenton is well known for her studies of moon astrology. In addition to a regular astrology column, she has published six books on the subject.

Druid Incantations - This incantation appears in Charles G. Leland's *Aradia, or The Gospel of the Witches*, published in 1899.

Anne Sexton - Imaginative and surrealistic, Sexton's poetry is often associated with the confessional school, which includes her friend Sylvia Plath. Her troubled life ended in suicide in 1974.

Frederick Adams - In *Hesperian Life and the Maiden Way*, from which these excerpts are taken, Adams hoped to undermine patriarchal dominance through celebration of the Goddess.

Zsuzsanna Budapest - Budapest is well known for her feminist witchcraft. She is currently the director of the Women's Spirituality Forum.

Homer - Little is known about the presumed author of *The Iliad* and *The Odyssey*. The Homeric hymns were used primarily as preludes to epic poems.

Joseph Campbell - Campbell is world-renowned for his writings on mythology. In this excerpt from *The Masks of God*, he discusses the lure of the moon, both tangible and abstract.

Norse Myth - This excerpt is from *The Prose Edda of Snorri Sturluson*, an ancient collection of Scandinavian poetry, incorporating the national mythology.

Carolyn McVickar Edwards - McVickar Edwards here recounts the often forgotten story of Adam's first wife. This story is excerpted from *The Storyteller's Goddess*.

Starhawk - These rituals can be found in *The Spiral Dance* (1979), Starhawk's influential and popular guide to the rebirth of goddess wisdom.

Chinese Legend - There are thousands of moon legends. This ancient tale demonstrates the romantic relationship between the sun and the moon evident here.

Ancient Myth - The myth of Endymion and Selene, retold here by Gayley, has been the subject of many writers, including Disraeli and Keats.

Ben Jonson - During the reign of England's James I, Jonson's literary prestige and influence were unrivaled. He was mostly famous for a series of realistic comedies.

Santería Fertility Rites - The relationship between the moon goddess and fertility is not uncommon. This excerpt is from a present-day Santería ritual.

Tess Gallagher - This poem from the 1992 collection *Moon Crossing Bridge* is dedicated to her late husband, Raymond Carver. Gallagher makes her home in Washington.

Pre-Hellenic Myth (Triad) - In many ancient cultures, including Pre-Hellenic, it has been suggested that as the Goddess declined, her characteristics were split into separate, weaker deities.

Apuleius - The most famous work of the North African rhetorician Apuleius (c. A.D. 125–170) was *The Golden Ass*, from which this scene is excerpted.

Emily Dickinson - Dickinson lived a reclusive life from her mid-twenties until her death in 1886. Of her more than two thousand poems, only seven are known to have been published during her lifetime.

The Book of Revelation - The final book of the New Testament, *The Book of Revelation* tells the tale of the apocalypse through the eyes of a dreamer, St. John.

Rig Veda - While goddesses play important roles in later Hinduism, most of the hymns of the *Rig Veda* are devoted to male gods. This excerpt is a rarity.

Henry David Thoreau - In this and other selections from *The Moon*, Thoreau often found that contemplation was best achieved during nocturnal wanderings.

Princess Enheduanna - In the ancient Near East, the city of Ur was dedicated to the moon. The principal deities of this city were female.

Sylvia Plath - Like her friend and contemporary Anne Sexton, Plath's poems were often painful. "Last Words" appears in her collection *Ariel*, published after her 1963 suicide.

Taranatha - This excerpt appears in *Tara Tantra*, written by Taranatha, the great historian of Tibetan Buddhism.

The Goddess Tara is considered the most popular deity of Tibetan Buddhism.

Lady Mary Wortley Montagu - At an age when women were denied an education, Lady Mary (1689–1762) defied convention, travelled widely, and became a prominent member of London's literary and cultural community.

Percy Bysshe Shelley - Another of the great English Romantics, Shelley's troubled and tumultuous life ended in a freak drowning accident in August, 1822.

Pre-Hellenic Myth (Hera) - Hera's authority was diminished in later Greek mythology, but she still retained the Goddess-like attributes of the wise elder.

Marge Piercy - Piercy's poetry and fiction struggle against the sexual injustice she observes in contemporary America. "The moon is always female" is from her collection *Living in the Open*.

Navajo Creation Myth - Like the Pawnee, the Navajo tribe, living throughout the Southwest, shared the belief in a First Man and First Woman.

H.D. - One of the leading figures of the Imagist Movement, Hilda Doolittle (1886–1961) wrote the poems of *Helen in Egypt* after surviving the bombings of London during World War II.

Acknowledgments

"Last Words" from *Crossing the Water* by Sylvia Plath. © 1971 by Ted Hughes. Reprinted by permission of HarperCollins Publishers, Inc.

"The Exultation of Inannu" from *Ancient Near East, Vol. 2* by James Pritchard. © 1975 by PUP. Reprinted by permission of Princeton University Press.

"Nörfi" from *Prose Edda of Snorri Sturluson*, trans./ed. by Jean Young. © 1964 by The Regents of the University of California. Reprinted by permission of The University of California Press.

"The Moon Was But a Chin of Gold" from *The Poems of Emily Dickinson*, Thomas H. Johnson, ed. Cambridge Mass.: the Belknap Press of Harvard University Press, © 1951, 1955, 1979, 1983 by the President and Fellows of Harvard College. Reprinted by permission of the publishers and the Trustees of Amherst College.

"Moon Crossing Bridge" by Tess Gallagher. © 1992 by Tess Gallagher. Reprinted by permission of Graywolf Press, Saint Paul, Minnesota.

"To Night" from *Selection from Vedic Hymns, Rig Veda*, by David Smith. © by McCutchan Publishing Corporation, Berkeley, California 94702. Reprinted by permission of the publisher.

"The First Woman and the Gift of the Moon" from *The Storyteller's Goddess* by Carolyn McVickar Edwards. © 1991 by Carolyn McVickar Edwards. Reprinted by permission of HarperCollins Publishers, Inc.

"Moon Meditations and Rituals" from *The Spiral Dance* by Starhawk. © 1979 by Miriam Simos. Reprinted by permission of HarperCollins Publishers, Inc.

Excerpt from *The Goddess of the Moon* by Sasha Fenton. © 1994 by Sasha Fenton. Reprinted by permission of HarperCollins.

Excerpt from *The Moon is Always Female* by Marge Piercy © 1980 by Marge Piercy and Middlemarsh, Inc. Reprinted by permsission of the Wallae Literary Agency, Inc.

"Thetis is the Moon-Goddess" from *Collected Poems* by H.D. © 1940. Reprinted by permission of New Directions, Inc.

Excerpt from *The Masks of God* by Joseph Campbell © 1959. renewed 1975 by Joseph Campbell. Reprinted by permission of Penguin USA.

The moon is always female by M. Piercy © 1980 by Marge Piercy. Reprinted by permissoin of Alfred A. Knopf.

"Last Words" from *Crossing the Water* by Sylvia Plath © 1971 by Ted Hughes. Reprinted by permission of HarperCollins.